Get Set Go Phonics

Puss in Boots

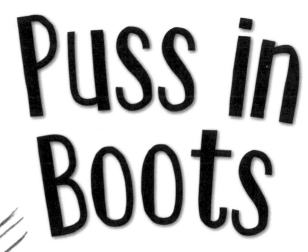

Phonics Consultant Susan Purcell

Illustrator Kay Widdowson

Concept Fran Bromage

Miles Kelly

Once upon a time, there was a miller who had three sons called Simon, Sid and Sam. When the miller died, he left the mill to Simon and his donkey to Sid.

Say the names as you spot each son in the picture.

Simon

Sid

Sam

2

Sam was left with the miller's cat, Puss. "Silly old cat, what use are you?" said Sam.

Imagine Sam's surprise when Puss replied, "Pass me a sack and get me some boots and you will soon see!"

Spot the word that doesn't use the s sound.

sand   sock   class   green

Focus on the k sound made by c and k (as in sack)

So Sam gave his cat a big sack and some red boots.

Puss put carrots in the sack and set off to catch a rabbit.

Sound out these words, which all use the k sound made by c and k.

car   coat   castle

keep   kick   jacket   luck

Puss went to the castle with his catch and presented it to the king, as a gift from the Marquis of Carabas. The king was delighted.

Say the words as you spot each thing with the **k** sound in the picture.

cat

buckle

king

5

The next day, Puss brought Sam to the river. Puss knew the king and princess would drive past soon.

"But I can't swim very well!" said Sam bravely, as Puss dragged him into the water.

Say the names of the things in the picture, as you spot them.

brick   bridge   dragonfly

dress   driver

"I might **dr**own!" shouted Sam.
Puss **dr**opped Sam's clothes behind
a **br**amble bush, just as the king's
coach **dr**ove over the **br**idge.

Spot the word that doesn't begin with the **br** or **dr** blend.

brush   brother   drum   hard

7

Try to hear the soft th sound (as in think)

Thank you for stopping!

Puss blocked the path of the king's coach.

"Thieves have pushed the Marquis of Carabas into the river," he shouted. "I think he's drowning!"

Sound out the words **thin** and **they**. Can you hear the difference?

Spot the word that doesn't begin with the soft **th** sound.

thin   thick   thorn   table

The king's servants threw Sam a rope and pulled him onto the bank. They fetched him clean clothes too.

Listen for the oo sound (as in boot)

Sam looked like a true Marquis in his blue boots. Then, the king asked him into the coach.

Sound out these words, which all use the **oo** sound.

glue   clue   flew   chew

soon   room   hoop

9

Draw attention to the h sound (as in happy)

Puss was happy his plan was working. He went up the hill and spoke to the workers gathering hay.

Spot the word that doesn't begin with the h sound.

hug   hop   hen   bat   hit

10

"Please say this is the Marquis of Carabas' land," whispered Puss to the workers, so they did.

The king was dazzled by this news.

Sound out these words containing the z sound.

zip   zoo   fizz   buzz

zigzag   these   cheese

11

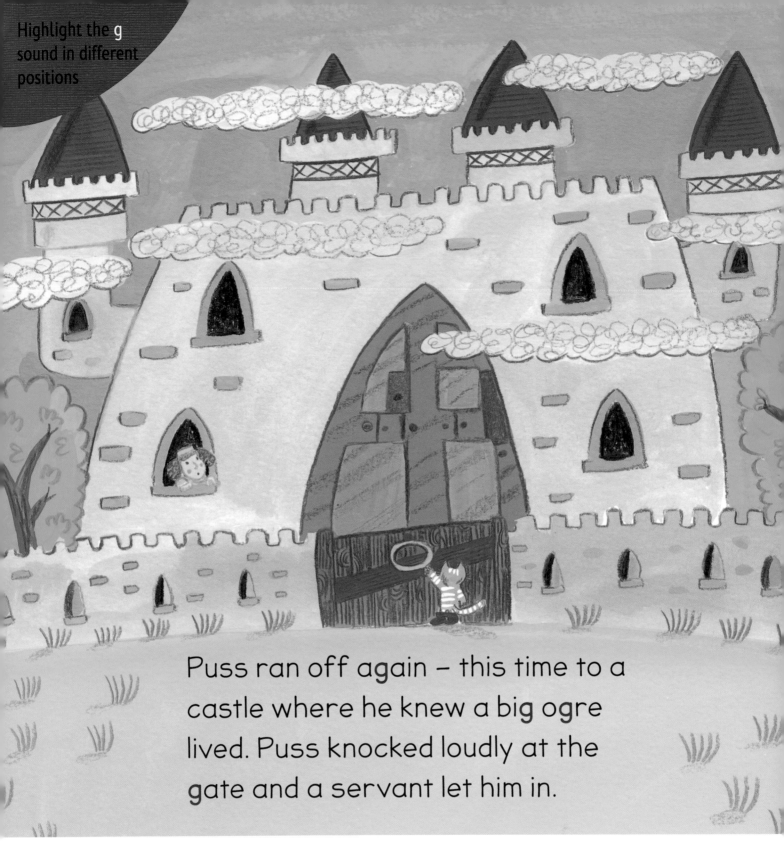

Puss ran off again – this time to a castle where he knew a big ogre lived. Puss knocked loudly at the gate and a servant let him in.

Spot the word that doesn't use the g sound.

goose   clap   buggy   egg

Puss was shown into the ogre's room and climbed up onto the oak table.

"So, what is it you need to know?" asked the ogre.

Emphasize the oa sound (as in oak)

Please show me some magic!

Sound out these words with the **oa** sound.

go   no   toe   note

goat   boat   grow   blow

Puss said, "I've heard you can turn yourself into anything you choose."

"Like something with fur?" snarled the ogre, as he turned into lion!

"Er... what about a little bird?" purred Puss. "Or a mouse?"

Sound out these words with the ur sound.

learn   earth   curl   nurse

girl   third   term   serve

14

Spot the word that doesn't use the **ur** sound.

early   church   star   herb

Sound out these words with the ow sound.

owl　　　how　　　town　　　flower

out　　　house　　　ground

The ogre growled, and in a flash he became a mouse!

"Now I've got you," shouted Puss loudly, and bounced down from the wall.

He pounced on the mouse, and that was the end of the ogre!

Emphasize the ow sound in the words as you say this sentence together.

"Now I've got you," shouted Puss loudly.

The servants in the ogre's castle were very relieved. They thought they would be under the ogre's spell forever.

We will be happy to serve the Marquis.

Sound out these words, which all have the v sound.

van   vase   wave

seven   velvet

To thank Puss, the happy servants organized a perfect party for everyone.

Focus on the p sound in different positions

Which food uses the p sound: grapes or cake?

Say the words as you spot each thing with a p sound in the picture.

cupcakes

Puss

apples

The next day, the delighted king offered the Marquis of Carabas his daughter's hand in marriage.

Sound out these words with the d sound.

dog   deep   dust   puddle

food   add   played

20

So, Sam the miller's son – now a Marquis – married the princess!

Draw attention to the m sound (as in miller)

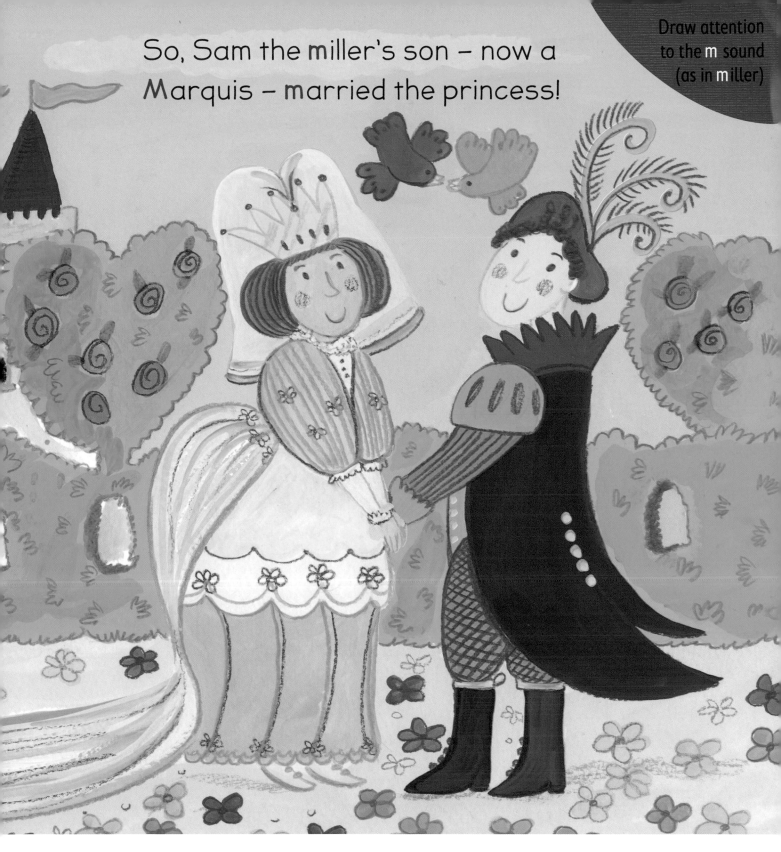

Spot the word that doesn't begin with the **m** sound.

mug   not   moth   mess

After that, Puss wasn't even expected to chase mice. He made himself an extra big pot of tea and sat down to relax!

Spot the word that doesn't use the **ks** blend.

exit   mix   box   wax   sick

Ask your child to **retell** the story using
these key sounds and story images.

Sam

Puss

sack

king

drown

ogre

mouse

marry

relax

Say the words in each line out loud together.
Can you **think** of another word that uses the highlighted **sound**?

bridge   brush   bramble   brick

thick   thank   thin   think

clue   room   chew   soon

hop   hit   hen   hat   hay

buzz   these   cheese   zip

big   goose   ogre   give

girl   term   curl   earth

van   velvet   vase   very

perfect   apples   happy   party

You've had fun with phonics! Well done.